MW00613578

Grant practices MATH with Manners

By Nadvia Davis, M.A.

Illustrated By George Franco

DEDICATION

In memory of my mother Ella Mae Davis
For O'ryan and Nyeshia

Today I used money from my piggy bank to buy my favorite cereal.

I can't wait to get home and pour my favorite cereal into a big bowl and watch cartoons.

Grant, let me take a look at your change and receipt. Grant hands his mom the receipt and money after buying the cereal.

Grant honey, the money you got back is wrong. Five dollars
minus three dollars is two dollars, not one dollar strong. You
need to go back and get it right.

Five fingers take away three fingers leaves two. Mom that's true!

You got this son. Just remember to use your manners.

But what if the words don't come out right?

8

Then you can say
you tried and
Mom will step in
and get things
tight.

9

10

So be brave and lift your chin, as you walk back to the cashier with a grin.

11

3.00

CEREAL PUFFS

12

Grant repeats out loud, manners in mind, always be kind!

Excuse me miss, my change is wrong. Five
minus three is two you see.
Can you please fix this for me?

15

19

Mom we did the math right and I was polite.

20

High five son!

Now we'll think about the importance of math and your sweet manners as we drive.

At first I was scared, but now I'm glad you cared to get it all squared away. You tell me every penny counts, now I know without a doubt.

That's right. Remember your manners will carry you
far, no matter where you are. Just be polite.

THANK YOU FOR SHOPPING!

26

The End

can be obtained
.ng.com
USA
14100720
V00003B/7